ZAHEER KHAN

INDIAN CRICKETER

MR VIVEK KUMAR PANDEY

Contents

Foreword

Short Biography Of Zaheer Khan & Life Style, Career etc. During Writing This Book No Character, No Religion & No Caste Are Harmed. It's Only For Study Purpose.

Preface

Author biography in English :

MY NAME IS VIVEK KUMAR PANDEY . I WAS BORN IN 30 SEP 2002,I AM FROM SURAT GUJARAT INDIA.MY DREAM WAS TO BE GOOD WRITERS ,MY FAMILY SUPPORTED ME TO SUCCESSFUL AND I CAN DO IT MY SELF.How do I write? That is a question, I believe, that can be honestly answered by me."CELEBRATING YOUNGEST WRITER AWARD WINNER IN GUJARAT 1ST RANK" MR PANDEY JI . I may think I did a good job writing something. The reader is the one who decides the quality of my writing. I do find writing to be natural to me and therefore find it to be a real challenge. My trick as a challenged writer is to do the best I can and know that I am happy with the final outcome. It may take a while to do my best and there may be quite a few problems I run into along the way.

I am not a greedy person those who are thinking about me and my self I never tried it anyone people suffering from sadness ,I trying to get promoted people suffering from happiness and joy in your Life Time. Now in current situation in India and also world people are unemployed and have no many but our indian governor help to people to get free food from ration card , i also take part in leadership team ,i am Motivational speaker , Film script writer. There was my two dream firstly writer and secondly actor & also my own film is upcoming soon i done almost completely completed script for my film .I AM GOING TO SAY WORD OF HEART TOUCH OUT PLEASE READ IT" , firstly i thanks my father he supports me in this field they always getting inspired me by own his words and behavior ,they always said that he was a biggest person in the world in future and also they purchase fruit and chocolate for me in anytime & anyway , firstly my father buy him then call me Vivek you want a chocolate i will say yes papa but how many tell me ,papa: you tell me how much i buy him i told 1 or 2 chocolate but my father purchase whole the boxes of chocolate and they get suprised me.

MY FATHER WAS BORN IN " 20 SEPTEMBER" 1971 IN INDIA.

1) MY FATHER FAVORITE CLOTHES IS KURTA PAIJMA AND ALSO STYLES SHOE

2) FAVORITE SINGER IS KISHORE DA

3) FAVORITE STATE GUJARAT AND KOLKATA , HIS VILLAGE IN BIHAR

4) FAVORITE COLOR BLACK AND WHITE

THEY ALSO LOVE cricket like IPL and one day t-20 .they also like watching a News daily and heard the song daily ,they also interested in tik tok video but in current time tik tok is banned in india but also few videos are in you tube. In lockdown time my family and me very enjoy day daily. my father play daily ludo with his sister and son, daughter.they always loved tea and coffee anytime call me "ı. I make it tea for my father but some reason after the April to june they are suffering from fever and cough , weakness on 6 June 2020 my father death. they not told me say bye bye his life. After death of 6 June on 10 june my mom and dad anniversary.but my father is Best in the world they can do anything for me please take care of father and respect it of your parents.

1

Zaheer Khan

Zaheer Khan

1. During Writing This Book No Character, No Religion And No Caste Are Harmed. it's Only For Study Purpose

Zaheer Khan (born 8 October 1978) is an Indian former professional cricketer who played all forms of the game for the Indian national team from 2000 till 2014. He is a fast-medium left-arm bowler. He was the second-most successful Indian pace bowler in Test cricket, behind Kapil Dev. Zaheer Khan started his domestic career by playing for Baroda. In the early years of his career, Zaheer Khan was known for his hostile seam and pace bowling, especially fast inch-perfect yorkers. He is often considered one of the best Indian fast bowlers.

In a bid to improve his bowling, Zaheer Khan moved to England for a short stint with Worcestershire in 2006. A left-arm fast-medium bowler, he was best known for his ability to "move the ball both ways off the wicket and swing the old ball at some pace". Zaheer Khan excelled in reverse swing with the old ball.

He is praised for his performances on flat subcontinent pitches and the controlling of different types of cricket balls. He was one of the key members of the 2011 ODI World Cup winning team, leading the pace attack with 21 wickets in just 9 games. In 2011 he was conferred with the Arjuna Award, India's second highest sporting award by the President of India. Zaheer Khan's career is also noted for recurring injuries, which often interrupted his progress at the international level. That is also the reason Zaheer khan has set up ProSport Fitness & Services, a special rehab & training center in association with Adrian Le Roux and Andrew Leipus. In 2020, the Government of India honoured him with the Padma Shri.

Zaheer Khan was selected as one of the Wisden Cricketers of the Year in 2008. Zaheer Khan announced his retirement from international cricket in October 2015. He also played for Worcestershire in County Cricket and played for Mumbai, Royal Challengers Bangalore, Delhi Daredevils and Mumbai Indians in Indian domestic cricket.

Only Muttiah Muralitharan (325) and Shaun Pollock (252) have dismissed more left-hand batsmen than Zaheer Khan, who has gotten the better of southpaws 237 times. He also has the distinct record of dismissing Graeme Smith, Kumar Sangakkara, Sanath Jayasuriya and Matthew Hayden – some of the game's most feared left-hand batsmen – over 10 times each in international cricket.

- Zaheer Khan Personal life

He was born on 8 October 1978 in Shrirampur, Ahmednagar district, Maharashtra, India to parents Zakia and Bakhtiyar Khan. He was born in a Marathi Muslim family. He has an elder brother Zeeshan and younger brother Anees. He started his coaching under Utsav Yadav. Zaheer attended the New Marathi Primary school and the K.J. Somaiyya Secondary School in Shrirampur. He also played in the local Revenue Colony Cricket Club (RCC) in Shrirampur after which he started his career in Pune.On 24 April 2017, he announced on his Twitter account that he was engaged to actress Sagarika

Ghatge. The couple got married on 23 November 2017.

- Zaheer Khan Domestic career

Khan came to Mumbai in 1996 and joined the National Cricket Club that played in Division A in the city. He played in competitions such as the Kanga Cricket League, Comrade Shield and the Purshottam Shield with the team. Sandeep Mahadkar, Khan's captain during the time, recalled the latter's ability with the ball with an instance where he reverse swung a ball that had been bowled 50 overs with, bowling ten maiden overs and helping his team win a Comrade Shield game. His ability with the bat was recalled by another former teammate with who Khan put together a 102-run stand for ninth wicket making an unbeaten 62 runs taking his team home. His "jaw-dropping spells in the Purshottam Shield" culminated with the 7/74 performance against Shivaji Park Gymkhana in January 1997. he was later sent to the MRF Pace Foundation in Chennai by Sudhir Naik, owner of the National Cricket Club. Impressed by his talent, the bowling coach there, T. A. Sekhar, pushed Khan to play for Baroda.

Khan quickly made his name playing for Baroda in the first-class level. In the final of the 2000–01 season of the Ranji Trophy against Railways, Khan received the man of the match award after he returned figures of 8/145 for the match, including a five-wicket haul in the second innings (5/16), helping his team lift the trophy for the fifth time and a first in 43 years.

Khan transferred to Mumbai at the start of the 2006–07 Indian cricket season his debut for Mumbai until the final of the Ranji Trophy in which he took 9 wickets as Mumbai defeated Bengal.

In 2005 Khan, signed for Worcestershire County Cricket Club in England as one of their two overseas players, replacing Shoaib Akhtar. Although Worcestershire went on to lose the match, Zaheer took ten wickets against Somerset on debut; in doing so he became the first Worcestershire player to take 10 wickets on debut for over 100 years. In June he took the first nine wickets to fall in the first innings against Essex, ending with 9–138; had wicket-keeper Steven Davies not dropped a catch offered by last man Darren Gough he would have become the first bowler ever to take all ten for the county.

Khan has played the Royal Challengers as well as Mumbai Indians before he was picked for the Delhi Daredevils in the 2015 auction. He has captained the Daredevils in 2016 and 2017. In 2017 season, Zaheer became the 10th bowler in the history and 8th Indian bowler, to pick 100 wickets in Indian Premier League. At the age of 38, he is the oldest player to achieve this feat.

• Zaheer Khan International career

Zaheer was selected in 2000 for the first intake of the National Cricket Academy in Bangalore. He made his Test debut against Bangladesh and ODI debut against Kenya during the 2000 ICC KnockOut Trophy in the same year.

In late 2005 pacemen Sreesanth and R. P. Singh made their international debuts and became regular members of the Indian team making it difficult for Zaheer to retain his position in the playing eleven. The Board of Control for Cricket in India demoted Zaheer from a B-grade to a C-grade contract at the end of the year. He returned for the 2005 tour of Pakistan, where India fielded three left arm pacemen and had difficulty dismissing Pakistan with a lack of variety in the bowling attack.

• Zaheer Khan Recall to team

Late in 2006, Zaheer was recalled to the Test and ODI team for the tour of South Africa, following Irfan Pathan's slump in form and an injury to Munaf Patel. After consistent performances on tour, his performance in early 2007 in home ODIs against the West Indies and Sri Lanka, including a career best 5/42, saw him named in the squad for the 2007 World Cup.

He won the Man of the Match award in the first Test between India and Australia in the 2008–2009 series in India for his all round performance with the bat and the ball.

· Zaheer Khan ODI career

He has taken 282 ODI wickets at an average of just over 29 runs per wicket taking 4 wickets in a match 6 times (4 times against Zimbabwe) including 32 wickets against Zimbabwe at an average of 17.46 runs per dismissal. He, along with other seamers like Javagal Srinath and Ashish Nehra helped India to make it to the finals of the 2003 World Cup. Zaheer finished the tournament as fourth highest wicket-taker – 18 wickets from 11 matches at an average of 20 runs per wicket. He is also the fourth highest wicket-taker in ODIs for India with 282 scalps behind Anil Kumble (337), Javagal Srinath (315) and Ajit Agarkar (288).

· Zaheer Khan Test career

Zaheer has taken 311 Test wickets at an average of just over 32 runs per wicket. South African star all-rounder Jacques Kallis was Zaheer's 300th test wicket. In 16 matches from the beginning of the tour of West Indies in April 2002 to the end of the 1st match against Australia in December 2003, Brisbane, Zaheer took 54 wickets from 16 matches at an average of 30 runs. It all turned downhill after the first Test against Australia in Brisbane in December 2003. Having taken 5 of the top 7 Australian batsmen in the first innings (5 for 95), he injured himself in the second during the opening spell. After missing the second Test he returned for the third, but was injured midway through the match and was forced to return home. The injury kept him from the early 2004 tour of Pakistan, India's first Test series victory in the country.

Earlier, Zaheer held the world record for the highest Test score by a number 11 when he scored 75 against Bangladesh in 2004. At the time he was batting with Sachin Tendulkar; the pair amassed 133 runs, a new record for India's tenth-wicket.This record was broken by Tino Best of the West Indies in 2012. The current record holder is Ashton Agar of the Australia on his debut match in 2013.

In international cricket, Zaheer Khan was the first bowler to bowl knuckle ball. Zaheer Khan introduced the knuckle ball way back in 2011 world cup. He used that ball for great effect. He used that ball to get crucial wickets at crucial times like the wickets of Ian Bell and Paul Collingwood against England and the wicket of Devon Smith against the West Indies and the wicket of Michael Hussey in the Quarter Final against Australia.

In an interview he said : "The whole 2011 World Cup, I was looking forward to it, especially playing in front of the home crowd – even if it added that extra bit of pressure. I was preparing a new delivery that I wanted to use, which was the knuckle ball. I was working on it for a year leading up to the tournament. Even though I had perfected it, I was purposely not using it in any of the matches. It got me a lot of success. When a plan like that works, it gives you extra satisfaction."

· Zaheer Khan World Cup

Zaheer has 44 World Cup wickets, spanning from 2003 to 2011, putting him in seventh place behind Glenn McGrath (71), Muttiah Muralitharan (68), Wasim Akram (55), Chaminda Vaas (49), Mitchell Starc(49) and Lasith Malinga (47) on the list of highest number of wickets by a bowler the marquee event. He is tied with Srinath in sixth but Srinath has played 34 games as opposed to Zaheer's 23. Zaheer, who was one of India's trump cards during their World Cup triumph in 2011, finished as the joint highest wicket-taker along with Shahid Afridi with 21 scalps.

· Zaheer Khan career

July 2011 India embarked on a tour of England. Having bowled 13.3 overs, Zaheer strained his hamstring and suffered an ankle injury in the first Test of the four-match series and as a result was ruled out of the rest of the tour. Zaheer came back in December and played a test match against Australia on Boxing day. He took two wickets in two consecutive deliveries, dismissing Michael Clarke for 31 and Mike Hussey for a duck. In the second test at Sydney, he took three wickets of the four to fall, Clarke scoring 329*; his were the best figures in both these innings. As of February 2014 Zaheer Khan is ranked 22 in the ICC Player Rankings for Test bowlers. He toured South Africa in December 2013 and New Zealand in 2014.

· Zaheer Khan Retirement

Zaheer Khan announced his retirement from international and first-class cricket on 15 October 2015 in a tweet saying "I bid adieu to my career in international cricket. I look forward to signing off with IPL 9."

· Coaching career

Zaheer was appointed as bowling consultant for the India national cricket team in 2017

In 2014 Khan founded a fitness and sports company ProSport Fitness and Services in Mumbai, that offers fitness training and physiotherapy services. Involving personnel such as Andrew Leipus and Adrian Le Roux, the center aims to "maximize potential" of people and athletes by personally assisted fitness programs. Khan stated that the objective was to "bring in world class fitness program to India for sports injury management". It offers scientifically designed programs and treatment while conducting workshops and sessions for corporates and schools to spread awareness of physical fitness.

2

Let's Know About Cricket?

- **Let's Know About Cricket?**

Cricket is a bat-and-ball game played between two teams of eleven players on a field at the centre of which is a 22-yard (20-metre) pitch with a wicket at each end, each comprising two bails balanced on three stumps. The game proceeds when a player on the fielding team, called the bowler, "bowls" (propels) the ball from one end of the pitch towards the wicket at the other end. The batting side's players score runs by striking the bowled ball with a bat and running between the wickets, while the bowling side tries to prevent this by keeping the ball within the field and getting it to either wicket, and dismiss each batter (so they are "out"). Means of dismissal include being bowled, when the ball hits the stumps and dislodges the bails, and by the fielding side either catching a hit ball before it touches the ground, or hitting a wicket with the ball before a batter can cross the crease line in front of the wicket to complete a run. When ten batters have been dismissed, the innings ends and the teams swap roles. The game is adjudicated by two umpires, aided by a third umpire and match referee in international matches.

Forms of cricket range from Twenty20, with each team batting for a single innings of 20 overs and the game generally lasting three hours, to Test matches played over five days. Traditionally cricketers play in all-white kit, but in limited overs cricket they wear club or team colours. In addition to the basic kit, some players wear protective gear to prevent injury caused by the ball, which is a hard, solid spheroid made of compressed leather with a slightly raised sewn seam enclosing a cork core layered with tightly wound string.

The earliest reference to cricket is in South East England in the mid-16th century. It spread globally with the expansion of the British Empire, with the first international matches in the second half of the 19th century. The game's governing body is the International Cricket Council (ICC), which has over 100 members, twelve of which are full members who play Test matches. The game's rules, the Laws of Cricket, are maintained by Marylebone Cricket Club (MCC) in London. The sport is followed primarily in South Asia, Australasia, the United Kingdom, southern Africa and the West Indies. Women's cricket, which is organised and played separately, has also achieved international standard. The most successful side playing international cricket is Australia, which has won seven One Day International trophies, including five World Cups, more than any other country and has been the top-rated Test side more than any other country.

- History of cricket to 1725

A medieval "club ball" game involving an underhand bowl towards a batter. Ball catchers are shown positioning themselves to catch a ball. Detail from the Canticles of Holy Mary, 13th century.

Cricket is one of many games in the "club ball" sphere that basically involve hitting a ball with a hand-held implement; others include baseball (which shares many similarities with cricket, both belonging in the more specific bat-and-ball games category), golf, hockey, tennis, squash, badminton and table tennis. In cricket's case, a key difference is the existence of a solid target structure, the wicket (originally, it is thought, a "wicket gate" through which sheep were herded), that the batter must defend. The cricket historian

Harry Altham identified three "groups" of "club ball" games: the "hockey group", in which the ball is driven to and fro between two targets (the goals); the "golf group", in which the ball is driven towards an undefended target (the hole); and the "cricket group", in which "the ball is aimed at a mark (the wicket) and driven away from it".

It is generally believed that cricket originated as a children's game in the south-eastern counties of England, sometime during the medieval period.Although there are claims for prior dates, the earliest definite reference to cricket being played comes from evidence given at a court case in Guildford in January 1597 (Old Style), equating to January 1598 in the modern calendar. The case concerned ownership of a certain plot of land and the court heard the testimony of a 59-year-old coroner, John Derrick, who gave witness that.

Being a scholler in the ffree schoole of Guldeford hee and diverse of his fellows did runne and play there at creckett and other plaies.

Given Derrick's age, it was about half a century earlier when he was at school and so it is certain that cricket was being played c. 1550 by boys in Surrey. The view that it was originally a children's game is reinforced by Randle Cotgrave's 1611 English-French dictionary in which he defined the noun "crosse" as "the crooked staff wherewith boys play at cricket" and the verb form "crosser" as "to play at cricket".

One possible source for the sport's name is the Old English word "cryce" (or "cricc") meaning a crutch or staff. In Samuel Johnson's Dictionary, he derived cricket from "cryce, Saxon, a stick". In Old French, the word "criquet" seems to have meant a kind of club or stick. Given the strong medieval trade connections between south-east England and the County of Flanders when the latter belonged to the Duchy of Burgundy, the name may have been derived from the Middle Dutch (in use in Flanders at the time) "krick"(-e), meaning a stick (crook). Another possible source is the Middle Dutch word "krickstoel", meaning a long low stool used for kneeling in church and which resembled the long low wicket with two stumps used in early cricket. According to Heiner Gillmeister, a European language expert of Bonn University, "cricket" derives from the Middle Dutch phrase for hockey, met de (krik ket)sen (i.e., "with the stick chase"). Gillmeister has suggested that not only the name but also the sport itself may be of Flemish origin.

- Growth of amateur and professional cricket in England

Evolution of the cricket bat. The original "hockey stick" (left) evolved into the straight bat from c. 1760 when pitched delivery bowling began.

Although the main object of the game has always been to score the most runs, the early form of cricket differed from the modern game in certain key technical aspects; the North American variant of cricket known as wicket retained many of these aspects. The ball was bowled underarm by the bowler and along the ground towards a batter armed with a bat that in shape resembled a hockey stick; the batter defended a low, two-stump wicket; and runs were called notches because the scorers recorded them by notching tally sticks.

In 1611, the year Cotgrave's dictionary was published, ecclesiastical court records at Sidlesham in Sussex state that two parishioners, Bartholomew Wyatt and Richard Latter, failed to attend church on Easter Sunday because they were playing cricket. They were fined 12d each and ordered to do penance.This is the earliest mention of adult participation in cricket and it was around the same time that the earliest known organised inter-parish or village match was played – at Chevening, Kent. In 1624, a player called Jasper Vinall died after he was accidentally struck on the head during a match between two parish teams in Sussex.

Cricket remained a low-key local pursuit for much of the 17th century. It is known, through numerous references found in the records of ecclesiastical court cases, to have been proscribed at times by the Puritans before and during the Commonwealth. The problem was nearly always the issue of Sunday play as the Puritans considered cricket to be "profane" if played on the Sabbath, especially if large crowds or gambling were involved.

According to the social historian Derek Birley, there was a "great upsurge of sport after the Restoration" in 1660. Gambling on sport became a problem significant enough for Parliament to pass the 1664 Gambling Act, limiting stakes to £100 which was, in any case, a colossal sum exceeding the annual income of 99% of the population. Along with prizefighting, horse racing and blood sports, cricket was perceived to be a gambling sport.Rich patrons made matches for high stakes, forming teams in which they engaged the first professional players.By the end of the century, cricket had developed into a major sport that was spreading throughout England and was already being taken abroad by English mariners and colonisers – the earliest reference to cricket overseas is dated 1676. A 1697 newspaper report survives of "a great cricket match" played in Sussex "for fifty guineas apiece" – this is the earliest known contest that is generally considered a First Class match.

- The patrons, and other players from the social class known as the "gentry", began to classify themselves as "amateurs" to establish a clear distinction from the professionals, who were invariably members of the working class, even to the point of having separate changing and dining facilities. The gentry, including such high-ranking nobles as the Dukes of Richmond, exerted their honour code of noblesse oblige to claim rights of leadership in any sporting contests they took part in, especially as it was necessary for them to play alongside their "social inferiors" if they were to win their bets. In time, a perception took hold that the typical amateur who played in first-class cricket, until 1962 when amateurism was abolished, was someone with a public school education who had then gone to one of Cambridge or Oxford University – society insisted that such people were "officers and gentlemen" whose destiny was to provide leadership. In a purely financial sense, the cricketing amateur would theoretically claim expenses for playing while his professional counterpart played under contract and was paid a wage or match fee; in practice, many amateurs claimed more than actual expenditure and the derisive term "shamateur" was coined to describe the practice.

- The Young Cricketer, 1768

The game underwent major development in the 18th century to become England's national sport.Its success was underwritten by the twin necessities of patronage and betting. Cricket was prominent in London as early as 1707 and, in the middle years of the century, large crowds flocked to matches on the Artillery Ground in Finsbury. The single wicket form of the sport attracted huge crowds and wagers to match, its popularity peaking in the 1748 season. Bowling underwent an evolution around 1760 when bowlers began to pitch the ball instead of rolling or skimming it towards the batter. This caused a revolution in bat design because, to deal with the bouncing ball, it was necessary to introduce the modern straight bat in place of the old "hockey stick" shape.

The Hambledon Club was founded in the 1760s and, for the next twenty years until the formation of Marylebone Cricket Club (MCC) and the opening of Lord's Old Ground in 1787, Hambledon was both the game's greatest club and its focal point. MCC quickly became the sport's premier club and the custodian of the Laws of Cricket. New Laws introduced in the latter part of the 18th century included the three stump wicket and leg before wicket (lbw).

The 19th century saw underarm bowling superseded by first roundarm and then overarm bowling. Both developments were controversial.Organisation of the game at county level led to the creation of the county clubs, starting with Sussex in 1839. In December 1889, the eight leading county clubs formed the official County Championship, which began in 1890.

The most famous player of the 19th century was W. G. Grace, who started his long and influential career in 1865. It was especially during the career of Grace that the distinction between amateurs and professionals became blurred by the existence of players like him who were nominally amateur but, in terms of their financial gain, de facto professional. Grace himself was said to have been paid more money for playing cricket than any professional.

The last two decades before the First World War have been called the "Golden Age of cricket". It is a nostalgic name prompted by the collective sense of loss resulting from the war, but the period did produce some great players and memorable matches, especially as organised competition at county and Test level developed.

• Cricket becomes an international sport

In 1844, the first-ever international match took place between the United States and Canada. In 1859, a team of English players went to North America on the first overseas tour. Meanwhile, the British Empire had been instrumental in spreading the game overseas and by the middle of the 19th century it had become well established in Australia, the Caribbean, India, Pakistan, New Zealand, North America and South Africa.

In 1862, an English team made the first tour of Australia. The first Australian team to travel overseas consisted of Aboriginal stockmen who toured England in 1868. The first One Day International match was played on 5 January 1971 between Australia and England at the Melbourne Cricket Ground.

In 1876–77, an England team took part in what was retrospectively recognised as the first-ever Test match at the Melbourne Cricket Ground against Australia. The rivalry between England and Australia gave birth to The Ashes in 1882, and this has remained Test cricket's most famous contest. Test cricket began to expand in 1888–89 when South Africa played England.

• World cricket in the 20th century

The inter-war years were dominated by Australia's Don Bradman, statistically the greatest Test batter of all time. Test cricket continued to expand during the 20th century with the addition of the West Indies (1928), New Zealand (1930) and India (1932) before the Second World War and then Pakistan (1952), Sri Lanka (1982), Zimbabwe (1992), Bangladesh (2000), Ireland and Afghanistan (both 2018) in the post-war period. South Africa was banned from international cricket from 1970 to 1992 as part of the apartheid boycott.

- The rise of limited overs cricket

Cricket entered a new era in 1963 when English counties introduced the limited overs variant. As it was sure to produce a result, limited overs cricket was lucrative and the number of matches increased. The first Limited Overs International was played in 1971 and the governing International Cricket Council (ICC), seeing its potential, staged the first limited overs Cricket World Cup in 1975. In the 21st century, a new limited overs form, Twenty20, made an immediate impact. On 22 June 2017, Afghanistan and Ireland became the 11th and 12th ICC full members, enabling them to play Test cricket.

- A typical cricket field.

In cricket, the rules of the game are specified in a code called The Laws of Cricket (hereinafter called "the Laws") which has a global remit. There are 42 Laws (always written with a capital "L"). The earliest known version of the code was drafted in 1744 and, since 1788, it has been owned and maintained by its custodian, the Marylebone Cricket Club (MCC) in London.

- Playing area

Cricket is a bat-and-ball game played on a cricket field between two teams of eleven players each. The field is usually circular or oval in shape and the edge of the playing area is marked by a boundary, which may be a fence, part of the stands, a rope, a painted line or a combination of these; the boundary must if possible be marked along its entire length.

In the approximate centre of the field is a rectangular pitch (see image, below) on which a wooden target called a wicket is sited at each end; the wickets are placed 22 yards (20 m) apart. The pitch is a flat surface 10 feet (3.0 m) wide, with very short grass that tends to be worn away as the game progresses (cricket can also be played on artificial surfaces, notably matting). Each wicket is made of three wooden stumps topped by two bails.

• Cricket pitch and creases

As illustrated above, the pitch is marked at each end with four white painted lines: a bowling crease, a popping crease and two return creases. The three stumps are aligned centrally on the bowling crease, which is eight feet eight inches long. The popping crease is drawn four feet in front of the bowling crease and parallel to it; although it is drawn as a twelve-foot line (six feet either side of the wicket), it is, in fact, unlimited in length. The return creases are drawn at right angles to the popping crease so that they intersect the ends of the bowling crease; each return crease is drawn as an eight-foot line, so that it extends four feet behind the bowling crease, but is also, in fact, unlimited in length.

Before a match begins, the team captains (who are also players) toss a coin to decide which team will bat first and so take the first innings. Innings is the term used for each phase of play in the match.In each innings, one team bats, attempting to score runs, while the other team bowls and fields the ball, attempting to restrict the scoring and dismiss the batters. When the first innings ends, the teams change roles; there can be two to four innings depending upon the type of match. A match with four scheduled innings is played over three to five days; a match with two scheduled innings is usually completed in a single day. During an innings, all eleven members of the fielding team take the field, but usually only two members of the batting team are on the field at any given time.

The exception to this is if a batter has any type of illness or injury restricting his or her ability to run, in this case the batter is allowed a runner who can run between the wickets when the batter hits a scoring run or runs,though this does not apply in international cricket. The order of batters is usually announced just before the match, but it can be varied.

The main objective of each team is to score more runs than their opponents but, in some forms of cricket, it is also necessary to dismiss all of the opposition batters in their final innings in order to win the match, which would otherwise be drawn. If the team batting last is all out having scored fewer runs than their opponents, they are said to have "lost by n runs" (where n is the difference between the aggregate number of runs scored by the teams). If the team that bats last scores enough runs to win, it is said to have "won by n wickets", where n is the number of wickets left to fall. For example, a team that passes its opponents' total having lost six wickets (i.e., six of their batters have been dismissed) have won the match "by four wickets".

In a two-innings-a-side match, one team's combined first and second innings total may be less than the other side's first innings total. The team with the greater score is then said to have "won by an innings and n runs", and does not need to bat again: n is the difference between the two teams' aggregate scores. If the team batting last is all out, and both sides have scored the same number of runs, then the match is a tie; this result is quite rare in matches of two innings a side with only 62 happening in first-class matches from the earliest known instance in 1741 until January 2017. In the traditional form of the game, if the time allotted for the match expires before either side can win, then the game is declared a draw.

If the match has only a single innings per side, then a maximum number of overs applies to each innings. Such a match is called a "limited overs" or "one-day" match, and the side scoring more runs wins regardless of the number of wickets lost, so that a draw cannot occur. In some cases, ties are broken by having each team bat for a one-over innings known as a Super Over; subsequent Super Overs may be played if the first Super Over ends in a tie. If this kind of match is temporarily interrupted by bad weather, then a complex mathematical formula, known as the Duckworth–Lewis–Stern method after its developers, is often used to recalculate a new target score. A one-day match can also be declared a "no-result" if fewer than a previously agreed number of overs have been bowled by either team, in circumstances that make normal resumption of play impossible; for example, wet weather.

In all forms of cricket, the umpires can abandon the match if bad light or rain makes it impossible to continue. There have been instances of entire matches, even Test matches scheduled to be played over five days, being lost to bad weather without a ball being bowled: for example, the third Test of the 1970/71 series in Australia.

- Innings

The innings (ending with 's' in both singular and plural form) is the term used for each phase of play during a match. Depending on the type of match being played, each team has either one or two innings. Sometimes all eleven members of the batting side take a turn to bat but, for various reasons, an innings can end before they have all done so. The innings terminates if the batting team is "all out", a term defined by the Laws: "at the fall of a wicket or the retirement of a batter, further balls remain to be bowled but no further batter is available to come in". In this situation, one of the batters has not been dismissed and is termed not out; this is because he has no partners left and there must always be two active batters while the innings is in progress.

- An innings may end early while there are still two not out batters

the batting team's captain may declare the innings closed even though some of his players have not had a turn to bat: this is a tactical decision by the captain, usually because he believes his team have scored sufficient runs and need time to dismiss the opposition in their innings

the set number of overs (i.e., in a limited overs match) have been bowled

the match has ended prematurely due to bad weather or running out of time

in the final innings of the match, the batting side has reached its target and won the game.

• Overs

The Laws state that, throughout an innings, "the ball shall be bowled from each end alternately in overs of 6 balls". The name "over" came about because the umpire calls "Over!" when six balls have been bowled. At this point, another bowler is deployed at the other end, and the fielding side changes ends while the batters do not. A bowler cannot bowl two successive overs, although a bowler can (and usually does) bowl alternate overs, from the same end, for several overs which are termed a "spell". The batters do not change ends at the end of the over, and so the one who was non-striker is now the striker and vice versa. The umpires also change positions so that the one who was at "square leg" now stands behind the wicket at the non-striker's end and vice versa.

• Clothing and equipment

English cricketer W. G. Grace "taking guard" in 1883. His pads and bat are very similar to those used today. The gloves have evolved somewhat. Many modern players use more defensive equipment than were available to Grace, most notably helmets and arm guards.

The wicket-keeper (a specialised fielder behind the batter) and the batters wear protective gear because of the hardness of the ball, which can be delivered at speeds of more than 145 kilometres per hour (90 mph) and presents a major health and safety concern. Protective clothing includes pads (designed to protect the knees and shins), batting gloves or wicket-keeper's gloves for the hands, a safety helmet for the head and a box for male players inside the trousers (to protect the crotch area). Some batters wear additional padding inside their shirts and trousers such as thigh pads, arm pads, rib protectors and shoulder pads. The only fielders allowed to wear protective gear are those in positions very close to the batter (i.e., if they are alongside or in front of him), but they cannot wear gloves or external leg guards.

Subject to certain variations, on-field clothing generally includes a collared shirt with short or long sleeves; long trousers; woolen pullover (if needed); cricket cap (for fielding) or a safety helmet; and spiked shoes or boots to increase traction. The kit is traditionally all white and this remains the case in Test and first-class cricket but, in limited overs cricket, team colours are worn instead.

- Bat and ball

Two types of cricket ball, both of the same size:
i) A used white ball. White balls are mainly used in limited overs cricket, especially in matches played at night, under floodlights (left).
ii) A used red ball. Red balls are used in Test cricket, first-class cricket and some other forms of cricket (right).
The essence of the sport is that a bowler delivers (i.e., bowls) the ball from his or her end of the pitch towards the batter who, armed with a bat, is "on strike" at the other end (see next sub-section: Basic gameplay).
The bat is made of wood, usually Salix alba (white willow), and has the shape of a blade topped by a cylindrical handle. The blade must not be more than 4.25 inches (10.8 cm) wide and the total length of the bat not more than 38 inches (97 cm). There is no standard for the weight, which is usually between 2 lb 7 oz and 3 lb (1.1 and 1.4 kg).
The ball is a hard leather-seamed spheroid, with a circumference of 9 inches (23 cm). The ball has a "seam": six rows of stitches attaching the leather shell of the ball to the string and cork interior.

The seam on a new ball is prominent and helps the bowler propel it in a less predictable manner. During matches, the quality of the ball deteriorates to a point where it is no longer usable; during the course of this deterioration, its behaviour in flight will change and can influence the outcome of the match. Players will, therefore, attempt to modify the ball's behaviour by modifying its physical properties. Polishing the ball and wetting it with sweat or saliva is legal, even when the polishing is deliberately done on one side only to increase the ball's swing through the air, but the acts of rubbing other substances into the ball, scratching the surface or picking at the seam are illegal ball tampering.

- Player roles

Basic gameplay: bowler to batter
During normal play, thirteen players and two umpires are on the field. Two of the players are batters and the rest are all eleven members of the fielding team. The other nine players in the batting team are off the field in the pavilion. The image with overlay below shows what is happening when a ball is being bowled and which of the personnel are on or close to the pitch.

- Return crease

In the photo, the two batters (3 & 8; wearing yellow) have taken position at each end of the pitch (6). Three members of the fielding team (4, 10 & 11; wearing dark blue) are in shot. One of the two umpires (1; wearing white hat) is stationed behind the wicket (2) at the bowler's (4) end of the pitch. The bowler (4) is bowling the ball (5) from his end of the pitch to the batter at the other end who is called the "striker". The other batter (3) at the bowling end is called the "non-striker". The wicket-keeper (10), who is a specialist, is positioned behind the striker's wicket (9) and behind him stands one of the fielders in a position called "first slip" (11). While the bowler and the first slip are wearing conventional kit only, the two batters and the wicket-keeper are wearing protective gear including safety helmets, padded gloves and leg guards (pads).

While the umpire (1) in shot stands at the bowler's end of the pitch, his colleague stands in the outfield, usually in or near the fielding position called "square leg", so that he is in line with the popping crease (7) at the striker's end of the pitch. The bowling crease (not numbered) is the one on which the wicket is located between the return creases (12). The bowler (4) intends to hit the wicket (9) with the ball (5) or, at least, to prevent the striker (8) from scoring runs. The striker (8) intends, by using his bat, to defend his wicket and, if possible, to hit the ball away from the pitch in order to score runs.

Some players are skilled in both batting and bowling, or as either or these as well as wicket-keeping, so are termed all-rounders. Bowlers are classified according to their style, generally as fast bowlers, seam bowlers or spinners. Batters are classified according to whether they are right-handed or left-handed.

- Fielding

Of the eleven fielders, three are in shot in the image above. The other eight are elsewhere on the field, their positions determined on a tactical basis by the captain or the bowler. Fielders often change position between deliveries, again as directed by the captain or bowler.

If a fielder is injured or becomes ill during a match, a substitute is allowed to field instead of him, but the substitute cannot bowl or act as a captain, except in the case of concussion substitutes in international cricket. The substitute leaves the field when the injured player is fit to return. The Laws of Cricket were updated in 2017 to allow substitutes to act as wicket-keepers.

- Bowling and dismissal

Glenn McGrath of Australia holds the world record for most wickets in the Cricket World Cup.

Most bowlers are considered specialists in that they are selected for the team because of their skill as a bowler, although some are all-rounders and even specialist batters bowl occasionally. The specialists bowl several times during an innings but may not bowl two overs consecutively. If the captain wants a bowler to "change ends", another bowler must temporarily fill in so that the change is not immediate.

A bowler reaches his delivery stride by means of a "run-up" and an over is deemed to have begun when the bowler starts his run-up for the first delivery of that over, the ball then being "in play".

Fast bowlers, needing momentum, take a lengthy run up while bowlers with a slow delivery take no more than a couple of steps before bowling. The fastest bowlers can deliver the ball at a speed of over 145 kilometres per hour (90 mph) and they sometimes rely on sheer speed to try to defeat the batter, who is forced to react very quickly.

Other fast bowlers rely on a mixture of speed and guile by making the ball seam or swing (i.e. curve) in flight. This type of delivery can deceive a batter into miscuing his shot, for example, so that the ball just touches the edge of the bat and can then be "caught behind" by the wicket-keeper or a slip fielder. At the other end of the bowling scale is the spin bowler who bowls at a relatively slow pace and relies entirely on guile to deceive the batter. A spinner will often "buy his wicket" by "tossing one up" (in a slower, steeper parabolic path) to lure the batter into making a poor shot. The batter has to be very wary of such deliveries as they are often "flighted" or spun so that the ball will not behave quite as he expects and he could be "trapped" into getting himself out. In between the pacemen and the spinners are the medium paced seamers who rely on persistent accuracy to try to contain the rate of scoring and wear down the batter's concentration.

There are nine ways in which a batter can be dismissed: five relatively common and four extremely rare. The common forms of dismissal are bowled, caught, leg before wicket (lbw), run out and stumped. Rare methods are hit wicket,hit the ball twice, obstructing the field and timed out. The Laws state that the fielding team, usually the bowler in practice, must appeal for a dismissal before the umpire can give his decision. If the batter is out, the umpire raises a forefinger and says "Out!"; otherwise, he will shake his head and say "Not out".There is, effectively, a tenth method of dismissal, retired out, which is not an on-field dismissal as such but rather a retrospective one for which no fielder is credited.

- Batting, runs and extras

The directions in which a right-handed batter, facing down the page, intends to send the ball when playing various cricketing shots. The diagram for a left-handed batter is a mirror image of this one.

Batters take turns to bat via a batting order which is decided beforehand by the team captain and presented to the umpires, though the order remains flexible when the captain officially nominates the team. Substitute batters are generally not allowed, except in the case of concussion substitutes in international cricket.

In order to begin batting the batter first adopts a batting stance. Standardly, this involves adopting a slight crouch with the feet pointing across the front of the wicket, looking in the direction of the bowler, and holding the bat so it passes over the feet and so its tip can rest on the ground near to the toes of the back foot.

A skilled batter can use a wide array of "shots" or "strokes" in both defensive and attacking mode. The idea is to hit the ball to the best effect with the flat surface of the bat's blade. If the ball touches the side of the bat it is called an "edge". The batter does not have to play a shot and can allow the ball to go through to the wicketkeeper. Equally, he does not have to attempt a run when he hits the ball with his bat. Batters do not always seek to hit the ball as hard as possible, and a good player can score runs just by making a deft stroke with a turn of the wrists or by simply "blocking" the ball but directing it away from fielders so that he has time to take a run. A wide variety of shots are played, the batter's repertoire including strokes named according to the style of swing and the direction aimed: e.g., "cut", "drive", "hook", "pull".

The batter on strike (i.e. the "striker") must prevent the ball hitting the wicket, and try to score runs by hitting the ball with his bat so that he and his partner have time to run from one end of the pitch to the other before the fielding side can return the ball. To register a run, both runners must touch the ground behind the popping crease with either their bats or their bodies (the batters carry their bats as they run). Each completed run increments the score of both the team and the striker.

- Sachin Tendulkar is the only player to have scored one hundred international centuries

The decision to attempt a run is ideally made by the batter who has the better view of the ball's progress, and this is communicated by calling: usually "yes", "no" or "wait". More than one run can be scored from a single hit: hits worth one to three runs are common, but the size of the field is such that it is usually difficult to run four or more. To compensate for this, hits that reach the boundary of the field are automatically awarded four runs if the ball touches the ground en route to the boundary or six runs if the ball clears the boundary without touching the ground within the boundary. In these cases the batters do not need to run. Hits for five are unusual and generally rely on the help of "overthrows" by a fielder returning the ball. If an odd number of runs is scored by the striker, the two batters have changed ends, and the one who was non-striker is now the striker. Only the striker can score individual runs, but all runs are added to the team's total.

Additional runs can be gained by the batting team as extras (called "sundries" in Australia) due to errors made by the fielding side. This is achieved in four ways: no-ball, a penalty of one extra conceded by the bowler if he breaks the rules; wide, a penalty of one extra conceded by the bowler if he bowls so that the ball is out of the batter's reach bye, an extra awarded if the batter misses the ball and it goes past the wicket-keeper and gives the batters time to run in the conventional way leg bye, as for a bye except that the ball has hit the batter's body, though not his bat. If the bowler has conceded a no-ball or a wide, his team incurs an additional penalty because that ball (i.e., delivery) has to be bowled again and hence the batting side has the opportunity to score more runs from this extra ball.

- Specialist roles

Captain (cricket) and Wicket-keeper
The captain is often the most experienced player in the team, certainly the most tactically astute, and can possess any of the main skillsets as a batter, a bowler or a wicket-keeper. Within the Laws, the captain has certain responsibilities in terms of nominating his players to the umpires before the match and ensuring that his players conduct themselves "within the spirit and traditions of the game as well as within the Laws".

The wicket-keeper (sometimes called simply the "keeper") is a specialist fielder subject to various rules within the Laws about his equipment and demeanour. He is the only member of the fielding side who can effect a stumping and is the only one permitted to wear gloves and external leg guards. Depending on their primary skills, the other ten players in the team tend to be classified as specialist batters or specialist bowlers. Generally, a team will include five or six specialist batters and four or five specialist bowlers, plus the wicket-keeper.

- Umpires and scorers

The game on the field is regulated by the two umpires, one of whom stands behind the wicket at the bowler's end, the other in a position called "square leg" which is about 15–20 metres away from the batter on strike and in line with the popping crease on which he is taking guard. The umpires have several responsibilities including adjudication on whether a ball has been correctly bowled (i.e., not a no-ball or a wide); when a run is scored; whether a batter is out (the fielding side must first appeal to the umpire, usually with the phrase "How's that?" or "Owzat?"); when intervals start and end; and the suitability of the pitch, field and weather for playing the game. The umpires are authorised to interrupt or even abandon a match due to circumstances likely to endanger the players, such as a damp pitch or deterioration of the light.

Off the field in televised matches, there is usually a third umpire who can make decisions on certain incidents with the aid of video evidence. The third umpire is mandatory under the playing conditions for Test and Limited Overs International matches played between two ICC full member countries. These matches also have a match referee whose job is to ensure that play is within the Laws and the spirit of the game.

The match details, including runs and dismissals, are recorded by two official scorers, one representing each team. The scorers are directed by the hand signals of an umpire . For example, the umpire raises a forefinger to signal that the batter is out (has been dismissed); he raises both arms above his head if the batter has hit the ball for six runs. The scorers are required by the Laws to record all runs scored, wickets taken and overs bowled; in practice, they also note significant amounts of additional data relating to the game.

A match's statistics are summarised on a scorecard. Prior to the popularisation of scorecards, most scoring was done by men sitting on vantage points cuttings notches on tally sticks and runs were originally called notches.According to Rowland Bowen, the earliest known scorecard templates were introduced in 1776 by T. Pratt of Sevenoaks and soon came into general use.It is believed that scorecards were printed and sold at Lord's for the first time in 1846.

3
History of cricket

- **History of cricket**

The sport of cricket has a known history beginning in the late 16th century. Having originated in south-east England, it became an established sport in the country in the 18th century and developed globally in the 19th and 20th centuries. International matches have been played since the 19th-century and formal Test cricket matches are considered to date from 1877. Cricket is the world's second most popular spectator sport after association football (soccer).

Internationally, cricket is governed by the International Cricket Council (ICC) which has over one hundred countries and territories in membership although only twelve currently play Test cricket.

- Origin

Cricket was probably created during Saxon or Norman times by children living in the Weald, an area of dense woodlands and clearings in south-east England that lies across Kent and Sussex. The first definite written reference is from the end of the 16th-century.

There have been several speculations about the game's origins, including some that it was created in France or Flanders. The earliest of these speculative references is from 1300 and concerns the future King Edward II playing at "creag and other games" in both Westminster and Newenden. It has been suggested that "creag" was an Old English word for cricket, but expert opinion is that it was an early spelling of "craic", meaning "fun and games in general".

It is generally believed that cricket survived as a children's game for many generations before it was increasingly taken up by adults around the beginning of the 17th century. Possibly cricket was derived from bowls, assuming bowls is the older sport, by the intervention of a batsman trying to stop the ball from reaching its target by hitting it away. Playing on sheep-grazed land or in clearings, the original implements may have been a matted lump of sheep's wool (or even a stone or a small lump of wood) as the ball; a stick or a crook or another farm tool as the bat; and a stool or a tree stump or a gate (e.g., a wicket gate) as the wicket.

- First definite reference

John Derrick was a pupil at the Royal Grammar School, then the Free School, in Guildford when he and his friends played creckett circa 1550

In 1597 (Old Style – 1598 New Style) a court case in England concerning an ownership dispute over a plot of common land in Guildford, Surrey, mentions the game of creckett. A 59-year-old coroner, John Derrick, testified that he and his school friends had played creckett on the site fifty years earlier when they attended the Free School. Derrick's account proves beyond reasonable doubt that the game was being played in Surrey circa 1550, and is the earliest universally accepted reference to the game.

The first reference to cricket being played as an adult sport was in 1611, when two men in Sussex were prosecuted for playing cricket on Sunday instead of going to church. In the same year, a dictionary defined cricket as a boys' game, and this suggests that adult participation was a recent development.

· Derivation of the name of "cricket"

A number of words are thought to be possible sources for the term "cricket". In the earliest definite reference, it was spelled creckett. The name may have been derived from the Middle Dutch krick(-e), meaning a stick; or the Old English cricc or cryce meaning a crutch or staff, or the French word criquet meaning a wooden post. The Middle Dutch word krickstoel means a long low stool used for kneeling in church; this resembled the long low wicket with two stumps used in early cricket. According to Heiner Gillmeister, a European language expert of the University of Bonn, "cricket" derives from the Middle Dutch phrase for hockey, met de (krik ket)sen (i.e., "with the stick chase").

It is more likely that the terminology of cricket was based on words in use in south-east England at the time and, given trade connections with the County of Flanders, especially in the 15th century when it belonged to the Duchy of Burgundy, many Middle Dutch words found their way into southern English dialects.

· The Commonwealth

After the Civil War ended in 1648, the new Puritan government clamped down on "unlawful assemblies", in particular the more raucous sports such as football. Their laws also demanded a stricter observance of the Sabbath than there had been previously. As the Sabbath was the only free time available to the lower classes, cricket's popularity may have waned during the Commonwealth. However, it did flourish in public fee-paying schools such as Winchester and St Paul's. There is no actual evidence that Oliver Cromwell's regime banned cricket specifically and there are references to it during the interregnum that suggest it was acceptable to the authorities provided that it did not cause any "breach of the Sabbath". It is believed that the nobility in general adopted cricket at this time through involvement in village games.

- Gambling and press coverage

Cricket thrived after the Restoration in 1660 and is believed to have first attracted gamblers making large bets at this time. It is possible, as believed by some historians, that top-class matches began. In 1664, the "Cavalier" Parliament passed the Gaming Act 1664 which limited stakes to £100, although that was still a fortune at the time, equivalent to about £16,000 in present-day terms. Cricket had become a significant gambling sport by the end of the 17th century, as evidenced in 1697 by a newspaper report of a "great match" played in Sussex which was 11-a-side and played for high stakes of 50 guineas a side.

With freedom of the press having been granted in 1696, cricket for the first time could be reported in the newspapers. But it was a long time before the newspaper industry adapted sufficiently to provide frequent, let alone comprehensive, coverage of the game. During the first half of the 18th century, press reports tended to focus on the betting rather than on the play.

- 18th-century cricket

Gambling introduced the first patrons because some of the gamblers decided to strengthen their bets by forming their own teams and it is believed the first "county teams" were formed in the aftermath of the Restoration in 1660, especially as members of the nobility were employing "local experts" from village cricket as the earliest professionals. The first known game in which the teams use county names is in 1709 but there can be little doubt that these sort of fixtures were being arranged long before that. The match in 1697 was probably Sussex versus another county.

The most notable of the early patrons were a group of aristocrats and businessmen who were active from about 1725, which is the time that press coverage became more regular, perhaps as a result of the patrons' influence. These men included the 2nd Duke of Richmond, Sir William Gage, Alan Brodrick and Edwin Stead. For the first time, the press mentions individual players like Thomas Waymark.

• Cricket expands beyond England

Cricket was introduced to North America via the English colonies in the 17th century, probably before it had even reached the north of England. In the 18th century it arrived in other parts of the globe. It was introduced to the West Indies by colonists and to India by East India Company mariners in the first half of the century. It arrived in Australia almost as soon as colonisation began in 1788. New Zealand and South Africa followed in the early years of the 19th century.

Cricket never caught on in Canada, despite efforts by the upper class to promote the game as a way of identifying with the "mother country". Canada, unlike Australia and the West Indies, witnessed a continual decline in the popularity of the game during 1860 to 1960. Linked in the public consciousness to an upper-class sport, the game never became popular with the general public. In the summer season it had to compete with baseball. During the First World War, Canadian units stationed in France played baseball instead of cricket.

• Development Laws of Cricket

It's not clear when the basic rules of cricket such as bat and ball, the wicket, pitch dimensions, overs, how out, etc. were originally formulated. In 1728, the Duke of Richmond and Alan Brodick drew up Articles of Agreement to determine the code of practice in a particular game and this became a common feature, especially around payment of stake money and distributing the winnings given the importance of gambling.

In 1744, the Laws of Cricket were codified for the first time and then amended in 1774, when innovations such as lbw, middle stump and maximum bat width were added. These laws stated that "the principals shall choose from amongst the gentlemen present two umpires who shall absolutely decide all disputes". The codes were drawn up by the so-called "Star and Garter Club" whose members ultimately founded the Marylebone Cricket Club at Lord's in 1787. The MCC immediately became the custodian of the Laws and has made periodic revisions and recodifications subsequently.

- Continued growth in England

The game continued to spread throughout England, and, in 1751, Yorkshire is first mentioned as a venue. The original form of bowling (i.e., rolling the ball along the ground as in bowls) was superseded sometime after 1760 when bowlers began to pitch the ball and study variations in line, length and pace. Scorecards began to be kept on a regular basis from 1772; since then, an increasingly clear picture has emerged of the sport's development.

- An artwork depicting the history of the cricket bat

The first famous clubs were London and Dartford in the early 18th century. London played its matches on the Artillery Ground, which still exists. Others followed, particularly Slindon in Sussex, which was backed by the Duke of Richmond and featured the star player Richard Newland. There were other prominent clubs at Maidenhead, Hornchurch, Maidstone, Sevenoaks, Bromley, Addington, Hadlow and Chertsey.

But far and away the most famous of the early clubs was Hambledon in Hampshire. It started as a parish organisation that first achieved prominence in 1756. The club itself was founded in the 1760s and was well patronised to the extent that it was the focal point of the game for about thirty years until the formation of MCC and the opening of Lord's Cricket Ground in 1787. Hambledon produced several outstanding players including the master batsman John Small and the first great fast bowler Thomas Brett. Their most notable opponent was the Chertsey and Surrey bowler Edward

"Lumpy" Stevens, who is believed to have been the main proponent of the flighted delivery.

It was in answer to the flighted, or pitched, delivery that the straight bat was introduced. The old "hockey stick"–style of bat was only really effective against the ball being trundled or skimmed along the ground. First-class cricket began, retrospectively, in 1772.A Game of Cricket at The Royal Academy Club in Marylebone Fields, now Regent's Park, depiction by unknown artist, c. 1790–1799

- History of cricket (1772–1815) and History of English cricket (1816–1863)

The game also underwent a fundamental change of organisation with the formation for the first time of county clubs. All the modern county clubs, starting with Sussex in 1839, were founded during the 19th century. No sooner had the first county clubs established themselves than they faced what amounted to "player action" as William Clarke created the travelling All-England Eleven in 1846. Though a commercial venture, this team did much to popularise the game in districts which had never previously been visited by high-class cricketers. Other similar teams were created and this vogue lasted for about thirty years. But the counties and MCC prevailed.

- A cricket match at Darnall, Sheffield in the 1820s.

The growth of cricket in the mid and late 19th century was assisted by the development of the railway network. For the first time, teams from a long distance apart could play one other without a prohibitively time-consuming journey. Spectators could travel longer distances to matches, increasing the size of crowds. Army units around the Empire had time on their hands, and encouraged the locals so they could have some entertaining competition. Most of the Empire embraced cricket, with the exception of Canada.

In 1864, another bowling revolution resulted in the legalisation of overarm and in the same year. W. G. Grace began his long and influential career at this time, his feats doing much to increase cricket's popularity. He introduced technical innovations which revolutionised the game, particularly in batting.

• International cricket begins

The first ever international cricket game was between the US and Canada in 1844. The match was played at the grounds of the St George's Cricket Club in New York.

• The English team 1859 on their way to the US

In 1859, a team of leading English professionals set off to North America on the first-ever overseas tour and, in 1862, the first English team toured Australia. Between May and October 1868, a team of Aboriginal Australians toured England in what was the first Australian cricket team to travel overseas.

• The first Australian touring team (1878) pictured at Niagara Falls

In 1877, an England touring team in Australia played two matches against full Australian XIs that are now regarded as the inaugural Test matches. The following year, the Australians toured England for the first time and the success of this tour ensured a popular demand for similar ventures in future. No Tests were played in 1878 but more soon followed and, at The Oval in 1882, the Australian victory in a tense finish gave rise to The Ashes.South Africa became the third Test nation in 1889.

• National championships

A significant development in domestic cricket occurred in 1890 when the official County Championship was constituted in England. Soon afterwards, in May 1894, the sport's first-class standard was officially defined. This organisational initiative has been repeated in other countries. Australia established the Sheffield Shield in 1892–93. Other national competitions to be established were the Currie Cup in South Africa, the Plunket Shield in New Zealand and the Ranji Trophy in India. The ICC re-defined first-class status in 1947 as a global concept.

The period from 1890 to the outbreak of the First World War has become one of nostalgia, ostensibly because the teams played cricket according to "the spirit of the game", but more realistically because it was a peacetime period that was shattered by the First World War. The era has been called The Golden Age of cricket and it featured numerous great names such as Grace, Wilfred Rhodes, C. B. Fry, Ranjitsinhji and Victor Trumper.

- Balls per over

During most of the 19th-century standard overs were made up of four deliveries. In 1889 five-ball overs were introduced in first-class cricket, with a move to generally use six-ball overs in 1900.

In the 20th-century, eight-ball overs were used at times in a number of countries, primarily Australia, where eight-balls were the standard over length between 1918/19 and 1978/79, South Africa and New Zealand. Since the 1979/80 Australian and New Zealand seasons, six balls per over have been used worldwide, and the most recent version of the Laws only permits six-ball overs.

- Growth of international cricket

Sid Barnes traps Lala Amarnath lbw in the first official Test between Australia and India at the MCG in 1948

The Imperial Cricket Conference was founded in 1909 with England, Australia and South Africa as the founder members. This aimed to regulate international cricket between the three sides, considered the only three of equal status at the time. West Indies were admitted as members in 1928, allowing them to play Test cricket against the other sides. New Zealand and India both became

Test playing nations before World War II and Pakistan joined soon afterwards in 1952.

At the initial suggestion of Pakistan, the ICC was expanded to include non-Test playing countries from 1965, with Associate members being admitted. At the same time the organisation changed its name to the International Cricket Conference. The first limited-overs World Cups were played during the 1970s and Sri Lanka became the first Associate member to be raised to Test playing status in 1982.

The international game continued to grow with the introduction of Affiliate Member status in 1984, a level of membership designed for sides with less history of playing cricket. In 1989 the ICC renamed itself the International Cricket Council. Zimbabwe became Full Members in 1992 and Bangladesh in 2000 before Afghanistan and Ireland were both admitted as Test sides in 2018, bringing the number of full members of the ICC to 12.

- International cricket in South Africa from 1971 to 1981

The greatest crisis to hit international cricket was brought about by apartheid, the South African policy of racial segregation. The situation began to crystallise after 1961 when South Africa left the Commonwealth of Nations and so, under the rules of the day, its cricket board had to leave the International Cricket Conference (ICC). Cricket's opposition to apartheid intensified in 1968 with the cancellation of England's tour to South Africa by the South African authorities, due to the inclusion in the England team of Basil D'Oliveira, a Cape Coloured player. In 1970, the ICC members voted to suspend South Africa indefinitely from international cricket competition.

Starved of top-level competition for its best players, the South African Cricket Board began funding so-called "rebel tours", offering large sums of money for international players to form teams and tour South Africa. The ICC's response was to blacklist any rebel players who agreed to tour South Africa, banning them from officially sanctioned international cricket. As players were poorly remunerated during the 1970s, several accepted the offer to tour South Africa, particularly players getting towards the end of their careers for which a blacklisting would have little effect.

The rebel tours continued into the 1980s but then progress was made in South African politics and it became clear that apartheid was ending. South Africa, now a "Rainbow Nation" under Nelson Mandela, was welcomed back into international sport in 1991.

• World Series Cricket

The money problems of top cricketers were also the root cause of another cricketing crisis that arose in 1977 when the Australian media magnate Kerry Packer fell out with the Australian Cricket Board over TV rights. Taking advantage of the low remuneration paid to players, Packer retaliated by signing several of the best players in the world to a privately run cricket league outside the structure of international cricket. World Series Cricket hired some of the banned South African players and allowed them to show off their skills in an international arena against other world-class players. The schism lasted only until 1979 and the "rebel" players were allowed back into established international cricket, though many found that their national teams had moved on without them. Long-term results of World Series Cricket have included the introduction of significantly higher player salaries and innovations such as coloured kit and night games.

• Limited-overs cricket

In the 1960s, English county teams began playing a version of cricket with games of only one innings each and a maximum number of overs per innings. Starting in 1963 as a knockout competition only, limited-overs cricket grew in popularity and, in 1969, a national league was created which consequently caused a reduction in the number of matches in the County Championship.

The status of limited overs matches is governed by the official List A categorisation. Although many "traditional" cricket fans objected to the shorter form of the game, limited-overs cricket did have the advantage of delivering a result to spectators within a single day; it did improve cricket's appeal to younger or busier people; and it did prove commercially successful.

The first limited-overs international match took place at Melbourne Cricket Ground in 1971 as a time-filler after a Test match had been abandoned because of heavy rain on the opening days. It was tried simply as an experiment and to give the players some exercise, but turned out to be immensely popular. limited-overs internationals (LOIs or ODIs—one-day internationals) have since grown to become a massively popular form of the game, especially for busy people who want to be able to see a whole match. The International Cricket Council reacted to this development by organising the first Cricket World Cup in England in 1975, with all the Test-playing nations taking part.

- Analytic and graphic technology

Limited-overs cricket increased television ratings for cricket coverage. Innovative techniques introduced in coverage of limited-over matches were soon adopted for Test coverage. The innovations included presentation of in-depth statistics and graphical analysis, placing miniature cameras in the stumps, multiple usage of cameras to provide shots from several locations around the ground, high-speed photography and computer graphics technology enabling television viewers to study the course of a delivery and help them understand an umpire's decision.

In 1992, the use of a third umpire to adjudicate run-out appeals with television replays was introduced in the Test series between South Africa and India. The third umpire's duties have subsequently expanded to include decisions on other aspects of play such as stumpings, catches and boundaries. From 2011, the third umpire was being called upon to moderate review of umpires' decisions, including lbw, with the aid of virtual-reality tracking technologies (e.g., Hawk-Eye and Hot Spot), though such measures still could not free some disputed decisions from heated controversy.

- 21st-century cricket

In June 2001, the ICC introduced a "Test Championship Table" and, in October 2002, a "One-day International Championship Table". As indicated by ICC rankings, the various cricket formats have continued to be a major competitive sport in most former British Empire countries, notably the Indian subcontinent, and new participants including the Netherlands. In 2017, the number of countries with full ICC membership was increased to twelve by the addition of Afghanistan and Ireland.

The ICC expanded its development programme, aiming to produce more national teams capable of competing at the various formats. Development efforts are focused on African and Asian nations, and on the United States. In 2004, the ICC Intercontinental Cup brought first-class cricket to 12 nations, mostly for the first time. Cricket's newest innovation is Twenty20, essentially an evening entertainment. It has so far enjoyed enormous popularity and has attracted large attendances at matches as well as good TV audience ratings. The inaugural ICC Twenty20 World Cup tournament was held in 2007. The formation of Twenty20 leagues in India – the unofficial Indian Cricket League, which started in 2007, and the official Indian Premier League, starting in 2008 – raised much speculation in the cricketing press about their effect on the future of cricket.

- thank you for buy & read this book

have a great day of your
from : Mr Vivek Kumar Pandey

- This All Credit Goes To My Super Hero Daddy. "Always Love You dad'.

41

- This All Credit Goes To My Super Hero Daddy. "Always Love You dad'.